For Goodness's Sake

Jackie J. McAdoo

Contents

Chapter One

What a beautiful day this was! Two little girls who lived together on Diverse Street loved each other very much. How could they not? They are identical twins and, therefore, mirror images of each other.

They looked so much alike that many people found it impossible to tell one from the other. The twins felt they looked very similar, but they were often amused by the confusion, embarrassment, and frustration many people said they experienced when trying to differentiate between them. People's expressions of exasperation were so hilarious to the twins that they could do nothing but laugh. Life in their little family was great.

Even though the twins enjoyed playing with their younger sister and older brother, they had a special closeness with each other. After all, they'd been together before they were born, in the same crib after birth, and in the same places with the same activities as they grew.

They slept in the same room, shared the same closet and dresser, and wore identical outfits, hairdos, etc., daily. Come to think of it, no matter where they went or what they engaged in, they were together. They hadn't experienced life any other way.

Now, it did bother them a little when their older brother, Shepp—short for Shepherd—would go off to different places by himself. It didn't appear that he planned or looked forward to playing with them very often at all.

"How does he do it?" they wondered. "Isn't he at all upset or lonely? Doesn't he miss being with someone to talk with, walk with, and play with- all the time?"

However, they'd never heard him complain about it - or about anything else, for that matter. Nothing seemed to bother him. He seemed to take whatever happened in stride, but of course he did; he was supposed to, right? After all, he was the oldest—their big brother. Wow! This, they reasoned is why he could be alone and do so much more than they could; and that was that.

Shepp didn't even have to sit like they did to use the potty! The twins couldn't figure that out either. Their big brother had special powers. Even Mommy and Daddy expected more from him. He got to do a lot more things, and he'd get things the twins didn't get.

"Oh!" they groaned. If they could be their big brother for just a day or two! That would be the life, all right.

Chapter Two

Shepp was older than they were, and the twins were older than their little sister. However, they did not seem to get any benefits from that. Actually, it seemed to put them in a worse position than their little sister. She was the baby, and it seemed to them that she got all the attention, even a great deal of attention from them.

Their little sister was the cutest little girl you'd ever seen. The twins were shorter, thicker, and less dainty than their little sister. Little sister was long and thin with small lips and a little nose – keener than theirs, long eyelashes, thin long fingers and feet, less coarse hair, and a higher pitched voice. She was a little princess, or at least she was what the twins thought a little princess would be like. She was so delicate and so sweet. Neither of those words would ever be used to describe them—trust me on that! Smart, funny, talented, all yesses. But not delicate and sweet.

Little sister didn't look at all like them.

Most people agreed. They'd say things like, "Are you sure she is their sister? She looks nothing like her mother. In reality, she had more of their mother's features than the twins did. She had their mother's thin, long torso, long, thin fingers, dainty, narrow feet, etc. She didn't have many of their mother's facial features.

Yep, people who had not met their father made comments about not recognizing her as our mother's child, and of course, they made her sad; none of us liked that at all. Couldn't they imagine how unkind their comments were? We could only sympathize with her? Her nice-nasty stares, comments and gestures were clear signs of her indignation.

On the other hand, it was often the opposite for the twins. By face, they were almost spitting images of their mother, yet they were the likeness of their father in most other ways. They had his rounder figure, his thickness, his rough skin, and his short stubby fingers. Their older brother was a more balanced mixture of both parents. He looked like himself, but you could see his mother and his father in him. At least, that's the way most people we knew explained it. That was the way it was—the way it was supposed to be. And that was fine, right? Or was it?

Actually, it was not—not fine, is what I mean—especially since no one had asked them for their opinion anyway.

Chapter Three

One day, when the children were taking their baths, Shepp, that's right, their older brother, who was going to be seven years old in a month or two, refused to get out of the bathtub. He played at washing and scrubbing himself with such enthusiasm. He washed and scrubbed so much until the twins—who darted in and out intrigued with Shepp's unusual actions—tried to realize how this game he was evidently playing could be so appealing to him.

What really got to them was what he did next. He became extremely agitated, cried frantically and put up so much resistance, kicking and flailing his arms as his mother tried to calm him as she pleaded with him and tried to help get him out of the tub.

As a last resort, his mother unstopped the tub to allow the water to run out while Shepp furiously fought to keep the water inside the tub while he simultaneously continued washing himself. His mother looked like she'd been in a wreck when she finally got Shepp out of the bathtub, dried off, dressed, and calm. Surprised and puzzled, she asked Shepp why it was so important for him to stay in the tub today.

Reluctantly, Shepp replied, "I needed to stay until I got clean like Aleeya and Adeara. They're always clean, and I am always so dirty."

"Dirty? What in the world are you talking about?" his mother asked. "All of you were dirty, and now all of you are clean," she continued. Shepp showed his mother the dark skin on his hands and said, "No, Mommy; see, I am still dirty, and I want to be clean too."

Then, he began to beg her as he cried hysterically.

"Mommy, please let me get myself clean too – please!"

"Shepp, my sweet little boy, you are as clean as your sisters are right now," said his mother. "But, Mommy, look at me. The kids say I can't be the twins' brother because I'm dark like dirt! They call me the dirty one." Aghast, his mother screamed, "What? Oh No!" as she interrupted him, quickly pulled him into a tight, protective hug for a couple of minutes, and said, "Your skin is darker than your sisters', but that has nothing to do with dirt, my beautiful little boy. You are clean.

And whoever said that to you evidently did not know any better. When we've finished eating, Mommy is going to show you something to help you understand. Okay?" She was livid, but she didn't want Shepp to know it.

Chapter Four

At that moment, his mother understood he'd been hurt and was now very confused and upset about his skin tone. She'd never imagined it made such a difference to him because it made no difference to any of them. Without a doubt, she had to talk to him about it. He was feeling inferior in his own family and ostracized by others in his world. "What must he think of her?" she thought since she and the twins were about the same skin tone. Here it was. A moment she had not anticipated would come this soon.

Her son felt he was dirty. She wanted to scream and lash out against the mean individual(s) who had planted the weeds of self-contempt into her son's mind.

Her son, Shepp, had always been a beautiful, loving, intelligent, fun-loving, easy-going jewel of a boy. Why couldn't they say some of those things to him?

"How long had he felt this way?" she wondered. "Why hadn't she noticed signs of him thinking this way before?" she asked herself. One thing was certain, though; she had to help him understand; she had to explain it clearly and delicately to him. She would not allow him to go through this week with this misconception. As she prepared their meal, she worked out a plan to help her son know and understand that he was as clean as clean could be.

Chapter Five

Mother found four of her whitest pieces of cloth. She and Shepp sat down. With one cloth, she rubbed across the baseboard; the cloth was now dirty. With the second cloth, she rubbed the floors; that cloth was now dirty too. With the third cloth, she rubbed Shabby's head.

Shabby was their grungy dog, so of course, that cloth was dirty and hairy, too. With the fourth cloth, she rubbed Shepp's arm. They both saw the cloth was clean. She rubbed Shepp's legs, his arms, his neck, and his elbows, but the cloth was still clean. Shepp was puzzled.

He was dirty, wasn't he? Mother let him study each cloth, including the one that had rubbed different parts of his skin.

Then she said, "See, you're not dirty. You were born with skin a little darker than mine and the twins. Your dad's skin is a little darker, too." "What?" Shepp said softly. "I was born a little darker?" "Yes," his mother said. "Let me show you something."

Chapter Six

Shepp's mother pulled out a dark brown crayon, a brown crayon, a tan crayon, a bronze crayon, and a beige crayon. She was careful to pull out some bright and some dark shades of the same color. Then she drew a little boy on white paper with a round head, square body, etc., and traced him to make four others just like him. She then asked Shepp to join her in using the chosen crayons to color shade in each of them.

They talked about how beautifully each one looked in their different tones and how easy it was now to distinguish one from the other.

"Are either of these dirtier than the other?" she asked Shepp.

Shepp laughed and replied, "Momma, you just drew them and cut them out of the same paper. They can't be dirty yet." Shepp answered. Mother pointed to the boy who was shaded dark brown and to the one shaded brown boy and asked, "I suppose since this one is much darker than this one, he must be dirty, right?"

Shepp shook his head, "No." "Well, how about this little boy? she said, pointing at the one shaded tan-. He's definitely cleaner than the others, right?" his mother asked. Shepp looked at his mother in surprise, then realizing she must be kidding, he folded over with laughter as he answered, "Mommy, all of them are clean! They are not dirty — they are all just different colors."

"What? They're just different colors?" she asked. "Do you mean neither of them is dirtier than the other—kinda like you and your sisters are different colors?" his mother questioned.

"Oh, like I am brown, and Aleeya and Adeara are … are…" Shepp was trying to figure out what color he should call his sisters.

"Different shades—like these little paper guys?" Mother chimed in quickly before Shepp could answer. "You've got it!" She realized Shepp was not fully on board yet. "Hey, Shepp," Mom went on, "Suppose we had cut some rounder or and some thinner – or longer; which would need to clean himself before the others could play with him?"

Shepp jumped up cradled his head in his mother's chest, flopped his arms around her neck and yelled, "Mommy, they are all clean! They all came from the same paper. They are just different colors!"

"Really?" his mother asked as though she hadn't already known.

"So, is any one of them better or nicer or cleaner than the other one?" Mom inquired.

"Unh, Unh, Mommy. No." Shepp shook his head but answered hesitantly.

"But, Mommy, why couldn't we all be the same color so people would know we're the same? I want to look like Aleeya and Adeara."

His mother raised her eyebrows and answered, "No, I don't know if that would work."

"Hunh? Why not? I think it would make everybody feel better if they looked the same," Shepp mumbled.

Mother answered, "Let's check it out and see if we could figure that out tomorrow, okay?" "Okay," said Shepp.

"We'll check it out tomorrow."

Chapter Seven

Uh-oh. The time has come—tomorrow is the day. This question she hoped she'd never have to tackle had just been raised and would have to be addressed tomorrow. "Wow!" she thought. "That little boy of mine is a bright little thinker, isn't he? This is going to be a little more difficult than I thought," Shepp's Mom nervously thought to herself.

She often questioned whether or not he would have to deal with the ugliness and pain of prejudgment so early in his life. She also wondered what the catalyst would be that prompted it. What would it do to him? How would he react? What could she do to prepare him?

"What kind of mother have I been?" she thought sadly. She shook herself and decided that the most important thing now was to help her son to love and be happy with who he was and how he looked.

It was going to be one of the hardest things she'd ever done because if the truth be told, she still thought about previous feelings of inadequacy and unacceptance that she'd had growing up. She knew this whole attempt at explaining could actually blow up in her face if she didn't do it right. She wanted Shepp to love himself even when other people did not. Somehow, she'd have to help him understand that there would be some people who would NOT.

UGH!

"Maybe she should let his father deal with it when he returns home," she argued with herself, but no. That wouldn't be for another week, and her telephone conversation with Shepp's father last night made it clear that his father felt Shepp would figure it out and make the necessary concessions to deal with it just as his father had had to do; with the hurts, the bitterness, the anger and all. She had to try to shape Shepp's outlook about this and similar issues regarding differences in a lighter, slighter, and less damaging way.

She prayed for help. She asked God to guide her - to give her the right words to say - the right things to do - in just the right way to restore her son's love of himself and to help him develop positive views of differences he'd find in life.

She had an idea. It was a Godsend, and why not? After all, this diversity began with God anyway. And God said, "It is good!" didn't HE? So, Shepp's mother took the day off from work.

Chapter Eight

Their mother put it all together while the children were at preschool and school. She made cutouts of trees, flowers, buildings, and people.

On one side of the table, she placed all the trees and people cutouts that were the same sizes, shapes, thicknesses, textures, etc., with no color or anything that one could use to differentiate them. She placed the cutouts, which varied in shape, size, color, texture, thickness, etc., on the other side of the table.

She also collected all the other necessary supplies and placed them on the table. She heartily prayed again, asking God's intervention to help her say the right things and for the children to easily get the message behind all this while she waited for the time to pick up her children – the treasures of her heart and bring them home.

She felt confident that her explanation would be clearer through the use of the objects in her hands-on illustration. She had her work cut out for her, though. She wanted Shepp to see and agree that diversity is what makes the world so beautiful and exciting. "Will he get it? Will they all kinda understand?" she pondered. "I certainly hope so," she said to herself.

Hours later, Mom went into action after Shepp and the twins came home. "This has to work!" she exclaimed as she called her family to the table full of supplies. They came in rushing, too. Upon entering the house, they'd seen what looked like the makings of a really fun afternoon, so they were very excited that it was finally time for their "fun time" to begin. Little did they know there was an educational purpose for it all.

Once everyone was seated according to Mom's directions, she let them know they were going to make two dioramas of a little neighborhood they'd like to live in.

Of course, she had to explain what a diorama was, show them a few examples, and answer their questions about it before they could begin. Once she was sure they understood their task — she explained that the items on one side of the table were to be used for one diorama, and the items on the other side of the table were to be used for the other diorama.

Mom insisted that they all begin working on the diorama using the same-shaped, same-sized people and objects she'd cut out - all made with the same pale paper.

Needless to say, their excitement waned as they picked up bland piece after bland piece, argued that certain pieces belonged to one or the other of them because they had been previously handled and purposed for placement by one or the other — of course, they agreed, they could not really tell — as they kept shouting how difficult it was to tell because they all looked exactly the same.

As Mom helped the diorama take on some definition as a place where people lived, they kept questioning who would want to live there because every street, every building, every person looked the same. "How would you know who your friends or your parents were — or even where you lived?" they repeatedly argued.

"It is so confusing and frustrating. And it's boring too! Who would want to live there?" one or the other of them retorted.

"Well, let's work on the other diorama for a while," Mom said finally. They were happy to do it because the variety of colors, shapes, sizes, etc., sparked their interest again.

Shortly after starting, they were laughing and yelling about how pretty one item or the other was as they made individual choices of particular trees, buildings, and people to live or interact with in one place or another in that diorama.

Mom heard them say things like, I'm going to call him one thing and him something else. They began to talk about how nice their part of the neighborhood looked and how much fun they'd have at this place or that. Mom stopped to ask if they wanted to return to working on the other diorama.

"NO!' they rushed to shout. "We like this one! See how nice it looks. We all have different houses and yards and people we play with."

Mom said, "Well, you could live in different places in the other diorama, too, couldn't you?"

"We don't like that one, Mom!"

"Really? Why not?" Mom asked.

"It is boring and confusing. We

wouldn't be able to tell who we were really talking to," said Adeara.

"We'd never be able to find our way back home if we left home. Hahaha! We could be right in front of our house and not even know it. And how could I identify my friends?" Shepp chimed in.

Aleeya sighed, "And it doesn't look pretty, or exciting, or fun either. I think I'd be scared of almost everyone there because I wouldn't be able to recognize my friends and family and…"

"Good gracious!" Adeara shouted uncontrollably as she interrupted her sister, "What about our food, pets, and other animals?"

"Calm down, calm down," Mother joined in saying. So, neither of you would want to live there now or visit? Mom faked perplexity as Adeara continued her audible rationale: "Nobody could live like that for long! You'd go crazy! "

The children were so piqued by how ridiculous the concept of everything being the same was to them that they discussed it a while longer with laughter at some points, sadness at other points, and a bit of fear, too, as they calmed. Mom heard them repeat phrases like, it would be too hard, too scary, so ugly, so dull, no fun, just awful, etc. Happy to see and hear them so engaged with the topic, Mom smirked and almost sang, "It's getting late, so let's wash and get ready for dinner.

After dinner, Mom asked them if there was anything they could do to make the first diorama a place they'd like to live in. They thought and said — "Make different kinds of trees and plants." Make the houses different; there are too many that look the same. Some of them should be small, and some should be tall, and some should be wide," one said. "Yeah, some should have shingles and some should have bricks," said another.

"They need to be different colors, too." Can we get some different trees and plants.

Everybody knows we need flowers with different colors and different shapes." "So you think making those changes would make living there better?" Mom questioned.

Their voices rang out, "Yes!" Adeara yelled, "That's what makes it beautiful and fun!"

"Well, who decides which ones will be big or small or brown or light green or pink or red or short or tall, anyway?" Mother asked.

Since this family regularly attends Church, Sunday School, and Bible study, it is no wonder that the children yelled out, "God, that's who!"

"So why do you think God made us and everything HE made look different the way we do," Mom's query continued.

Shepp was the first to answer, "So we could tell each other apart, be able to tell where we are and where we live, and it is a happier place because it's so exciting and wonderful."

"But, if someone or something is short and wants to be tall, or if they are one shade and they want to be another, then what?" Mom asked.

"Aleeya yelled, "They must not understand! They cannot go changing things over and over once things are the way they are. That would make us more confused."

With a smirk, Adeara said, "God was smart enough to make the world with different shapes and colors and stuff like the second diorama, so I'm sure HE knew the best way to do it, too!

And I'll bet HE didn't have to make two dioramas to figure it out either!" They all screamed,

"That's right!" and laughed loudly as they happily agreed.

"Okay, my beautiful little ones, it's time for baths and bed," announced Mom. Needless to say, the baths were completed without a hitch that evening.

41

Everybody washed themselves, played in the bubbles, and got out of the bathtub, even Shepp. As Mom passed the bathroom and noticed Shepp drying himself and donning his pajamas, she said, "What? No fight tonight, Shepp?"

Shepp said, "No. Some people don't understand it yet, but God has how everything should be figured out already. HE wanted me to be here just like I am – and HE's real smart, so no matter what anyone else says about it, I'm sticking with God."

"Me too," his mother muttered as she continued down the hall.

She plopped down on her bed, gazed towards heaven, exhaled, and in a little louder than a whisper said, "Whew! Lord! Thank you. It sounds like Shepp is going to be alright – at least for now. Thank You for your intervention."

Made in United States
Orlando, FL
26 November 2024

54493756R00027